First published in the United States, Great Britain, Canada, Australia,
and New Zealand in 2005 by North-South Books, an imprint of
NordSüd Verlag AG, Gossau Zürich, Switzerland.

Distributed in the United States by North-South Books Inc., New York.

Library of Congress Cataloging-in-Publication Data is available.
A CIP catalogue record for this book is available from The British Library.

ISBN 0-7358-2005-8 (trade edition)
10 9 8 7 6 5 4 3 2 1

Printed in Denmark

Five days until Hedgehog comes home.

Every night at eight o'clock, we'll look up at the bright star just to the left of the moon. Then we'll think of one another.

In four days my trip will be over, and I will see Mouse again.
Today I wrote Mouse a letter and told her that I love her.
I sent it by airmail.
I wonder what Mouse is doing right now.

Four days left until Hedgehog comes home.

This morning I gave the dove a letter for Hedgehog. I wrote that I loved him. I hope he gets the letter soon.

Where could he be right now?

In three days my trip will be over, and I will see Mouse again.

Today I went walking and met two rabbits. They were quite nice, but they were strangely dressed. Perhaps I looked odd to the rabbits too? There is nobody to talk to about the rabbits. Without Mouse, this trip is not much fun.

Good night, dear Mouse.

Three days left until Hedgehog comes home.

Today I met a very nice hare. We played a game of hide-and-seek and it was lots of fun. But it would have been more fun if Hedgehog had been here. I wish he was.

Good night, dear Hedgehog.

In two days my trip will be over, and I will see Mouse again. I am bringing something lovely back for her. She has wanted it for a long time. I am sure she thinks that I have forgotten. But I could never forget.

I hope she likes it.

Two days left until Hedgehog comes home.
Today I listened to music. I heard the song that Hedgehog and
I always dance to. I'm so glad we'll be together again soon.
With Hedgehog, everything is always so much nicer.

Only one more day until my trip is over, and I will see
Mouse again!

Every night, when I look at the bright star to the left of the
moon, I think of her. Today I got a letter from Mouse–a letter
and a picture.

Tomorrow morning, I am going home. I will meet Mouse
at the train station. I think I am more excited than she is!

Until tomorrow, dear Mouse!

Only one more day until we're together again!
Tomorrow Hedgehog comes home. We'll meet at the station.
I'm so excited that I'm sure I won't be able to sleep!
Until tomorrow, dear Hedgehog!

"There you are, Hedgehog!" cried Mouse. "I waited at the flower stall in the station for such a long time, but you just weren't there."

"Oh dear Mouse, I am so happy to see you!" said Hedgehog. "When I could not find you at the newspaper stand at the station, I thought that you had forgotten me!"

"I've been thinking only of you for five long days," Mouse said.

"From now on," said Hedgehog, "we will always travel together."